E
BER   93-7697

Berenstain, Michael
When I Grow Up

Michael Berenstain's
WHEN I GROW UP

Oh, the Things I Can Be!

A GOLDEN BOOK•NEW YORK
Western Publishing Company, Inc., Racine, Wisconsin 53404

We are kids!
We run, we play.
We learn in school
and have fun all day!

That's our job—
it's what we do,
and we're pretty
good at it, too!

But . . .
When we grow up,
what will we be?
What are the best jobs
for you and me?

Carpenter? Painter?
Mail carrier? Cook?
Let's go for a walk,
let's take a look!

How about fire fighter?
We could do that—
ride on a fire truck
and wear a neat hat.

We could save people's lives,
or save someone's pet—
I hope they won't mind
if they get a bit wet!

A traffic cop's job
is to know
when cars should stop—
when they should go.

I like airplanes.
I want to fly!
Airline pilot's
a job I'd try.

Why just airplanes?
Really *go* someplace.
Be an astronaut—
blast off into space!

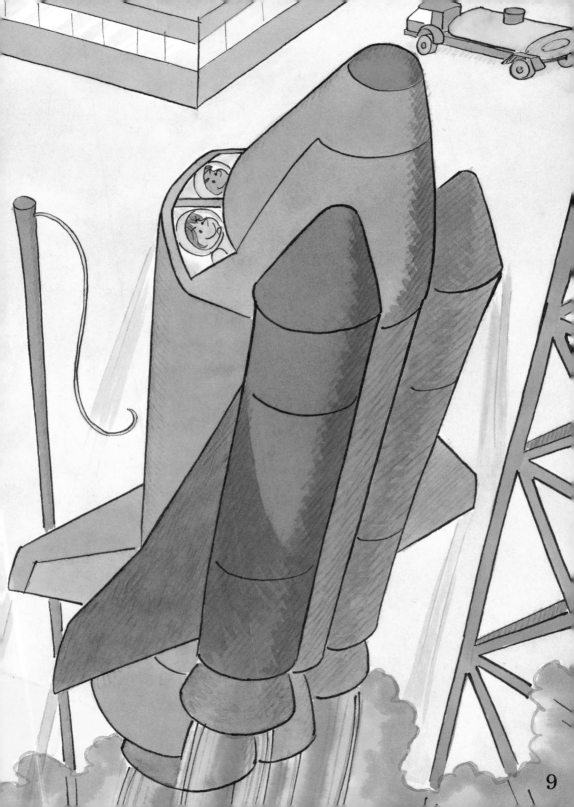

Maybe I should
stay on the ground
and learn to drive
a truck around.

I'll drive a steam shovel
that's very big!
Now, there's a job
I can really dig.

Cars, trucks, and planes
need lots of oil.
To get it we dig
deep down in the soil.

Oil rig workers
drill deep, deep wells
to get all the fuel
that a gas station sells.

GASOLINE

Bob's Service

If we could travel
way out west
to find the job that
we like best,
we might be cowboys,
or cowgirls, of course,
roping a calf
and riding a horse!

13

Farmers grow
the food we eat—
the rows of corn
and fields of wheat.

They plant and harvest,
weed and plow,
but still have time
to milk the cow.

I like the jobs
we've seen so far.
But that's not *all*
the jobs there are!

A teacher's something
I could be—
I already know about
three plus three.

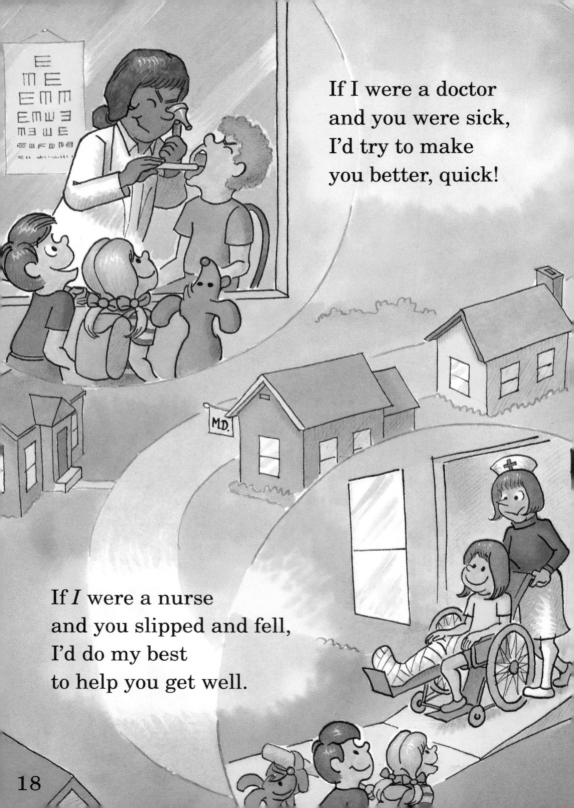

If I were a doctor
and you were sick,
I'd try to make
you better, quick!

If *I* were a nurse
and you slipped and fell,
I'd do my best
to help you get well.

Don't forget dentist—
it might be a thrill
to get on the *other*
end of that drill!

19

I like to learn about
plants and trees—
bugs and birds,
flowers and bees.

Then be a scientist
and study things—
how plants grow,
why a bird sings.

An artist's life
is the one for me.
You just need talent,
don't you agree?

My talent is dancing—
watch me pirouette!
I'll be a ballerina—
the greatest one yet!

I like to run
and jump and tumble.
I'll be an athlete—
uh-oh! *Fumble!*

Let's go to the circus—
what a fun place to be!
I think I'd even work
at the circus for free!

25

Now, here's a job
with lots of zip—
the human cannonball.
What a trip!

26

While over here,
in ring number three,
we have our new lion tamer.   Who, *me*?

I'll be a clown—
a funny guy—
with rubber feet
and a trick bow tie.

The jobs we've seen
sure look like fun!
But there's one more
for everyone.

This job's not one
that's done for pay,
but grown-ups like it
anyway.

It's the job of parent—
a mom or a dad.
A job that makes you
proud and glad.

When we grow up,
we may be parents, too.
Now, *there's* a good job
for me and you!